Marcus Donaldson lives in Northern Ireland with his wife and young family. In his spare time, he enjoys running and reading. He has always been a keen traveller and is happiest in the middle of somewhere like the ruins of Machu Picchu or the jungles of Myanmar.

For the real Max, who made sure this book was written.

Marcus Donaldson

THE BLACK KNIGHT AND THE VOYAGE TO THE DARK SEAS

AUSTIN MACAULEY PUBLISHERS™

LONDON • CAMBRIDGE • NEW YORK • SHARJAH

A CIP catalogue record for this title is available from the British Library.

ISBN 9781398436114 (Paperback)
ISBN 9781398436121 (ePub e-book)

www.austinmacauley.com

First Published 2022
Austin Macauley Publishers Ltd®
1 Canada Square
Canary Wharf
London
E14 5AA

Chapter 1

During the fiercest storm he could remember, the Black Knight left Cracked Rock Castle, his horse flinching at each flash of lightening and the thunder that followed. The road that led to the ancient castle was slick with rain, the cobbles making Bolt slip and skid as the Black Knight spurred him onward. He was heading for his fastest ship, the Dragon's Tooth, which was tied up in the busy harbour of the trading town at the foot of the Kings Road. The steep route wound its way down from Cracked Rock Castle to the town of Andover, which overlooked the deep waters of Andover Lough.

Sparing no time, the Black Knight galloped through the now quiet cobbled streets that hummed with activity during the day. More than one resident muttered a curse as they were woken by the clatter of hooves. Bolt surged up the timber gangway and onto the Dragon's Tooth, the Black Knight leaping from its back onto the empty deck. When he peered out of his cabin window that overlooked the deck, Captain Courtney spat out his tea in surprise and rushed out of his warm cabin and into the stormy night on deck.

"My Lord! I wasn't expecting you!" The captain brushed the tea from his tunic and ushered the Black Knight into his cabin. The captain hurriedly cleared some papers from his chair, but the Black Knight didn't sit. "Set sail immediately for the Dark Seas," ordered the knight as water ran from the obsidian black chest plate, greaves and vambraces.

"But…But, the storm My Lord, we'll be dashed to pieces on the rocks at the mouth of the harbour and even if we get past those, there's the whirlpools that guard the gates to the Dark Seas. They are ship killers at this time of year! Then there's the Fire Eels! We have no fire shields on board and…"

"Silence, Courtney," The Black Knight spoke quietly, holding up a gauntleted hand, stopping the captains garbling mid-flow. "There is no choice. Ring the bell and rouse the crew."

The Black Knight left the cabin as the crew bell began to peal. The door from the crew quarters sprang open, disgorging bleary eyed men pulling on canvas jackets and yanking hoods up in a desperate attempt to fend off the storm whirling and whistling about them. The first man out of the door saw the Black Knight striding to his horse and stopped suddenly, so that his mates behind bumped into him, throwing him forward. After the Black Knight had gathered his horse's reins and led it under cover at the back of the ship, his metal boots clanking on the wooden deck, the crew began to whisper.

"What's the Black Knight doing here on a night like this?!"

"This can't be good," whispered Old Pete as he buttoned his faded blue jacket.

"I reckon he's here to teach you a lesson, Smiffy!" One of the crew muttered to the last man out of the crew quarters, who was known for his laziness. Smiffy went pale with fright and began to shake.

"You men, stop gabbling like old women and get to work!" The first mate had come out of the captain's cabin and crossed the deck. "We sail in ten minutes."

The crew's mouths dropped. Smiffy went even paler.

Eight minutes later, the Dragon's Tooth put to sea in one of the worst storms anyone could remember. The ship was a square-rigged caravel with two masts. With a fair wind, the 60-foot ship could outpace almost any ship afloat and plied the trading route between Andover, the Fair Isles and the capital in Dronningen. Of course, not many trading ships had quite as many cannon, but the Black Knight believed it was better to be prepared.

In his large cabin, which the Captain had recently removed his belongings from, the Black Knight took his helmet off, unbuckled his sword and removed his shining black armour, piece by piece. The armour was carefully packed into a war box, covering each plate with a soft cloth. It had been forged by Dwarves from volcanic lava 1000 years before and had never lost its shine. The troll who had killed the dwarves and taken their mountain home had kept it as his prize for a hundred years before the Black Knight had fought him. When he killed the troll, the armour had become his. When he had tried it on, it had been much too small as it had been made for a dwarf, but it had magically reshaped itself to fit him perfectly. Dwarvish armour had long been rumoured to mould itself to a new owner who won it in combat. The armour consisted of a breastplate that was shaped to fit the Black Knight's powerful chest, vambraces that protected his forearms and vambraces that covered his

9

lower legs. The helmet was the final piece and fitted the Black Knight's head snugly, with pointed check guards that met beneath an extended nose guard. The armour was stronger than stone but so light that it allowed the wearer to move with ease. Under his armour, the Black Knight wore a simple black cotton tunic and trousers. On top of the armour, the Black Knight laid his longsword with its leather double handed hilt wound in filigree wire. The scabbard had been strapped to the Black Knight's back, meaning that he could move more easily without the hindrance of the long blade at his side. He kept the rondel dagger in his belt. Even amongst friends, the Black Knight never let his guard down.

The Black Knight unrolled the piece of paper that held the message which had started this journey. It had come to his castle tied to an eagles foot.

"Max, I have been captured. It's CJ. Dark Seas."

That was all the tiny note said but the Black Knight knew it was from his brother, The White Knight. The Black Knight recognised the handwriting, and, after all, only his brother would dare call him by his real name.

'CJ', which could only stand for Calico Jack, was a fearsome pirate who terrorised the oceans and was known to have a base somewhere in the Dark Seas, a terrible stretch of water where pirates, dragons, witches and more held power and no good people dared go. It could only be reached by the Black Gates; a narrow stretch of sea that ran between two high cliffs, each with a huge statue of an ancient warrior, warning seafarers not to enter with an upraised arm. In the winter months, huge whirlpools could spring out of nowhere, whisking a ship to its doom before anyone on board knew what was happening.

Chapter 2

When the Black Knight woke up the next morning, the Dragon's Tooth was approaching the Black Gates. The storm had eased and the sun had come out as the twin statues drew closer.

After he put his armour on and strapped his sword to his back, the Black Knight went out on deck. The Dragon's Tooth was entering the Black Gates, and the huge cliffs towered on either side of the ship. The crew scurried about their tasks, not speaking, and looking up at the walls of rock on either side. The wind died away and Captain Courtney had to shout.

"Oarsmen, to your benches!"

Within seconds the long oars slid out and began to pull the ship forward, deeper into the Black Gates.

"Captain, have buckets of water filled and put on deck. Soak everything you can see with water as well and tell the ship's doctor to get ready," the Black Knight ordered. He knew what lay ahead in the Black Gates.

"Get the crew armed and I want archers on either side of the ship," he continued.

The Captain, who had been standing beside the Black Knight nodded and began snapping commands to the crew.

The Dragon's Tooth continued along the gorge slowly. The people on deck could only see a narrow strip of daylight hundreds of feet above them, blue sky peeking between the cliffs that almost seemed to meet over their heads. The Black Knight stood on the forecastle behind the helmsman, watching the black holes in the cliff sides that marked out cave entrances.

"Watch out!!!" One of the crew screamed and suddenly an arrow thudded into the deck. Then, arrow after arrow whistled through the air, falling on the Dragon's Tooth.

"Get under cover!" thundered the Black Knight, as an arrow pinged off his armour. The crew dived for anything to hide behind, but not before Smiffy got hit in the leg by an arrow. The Black Knight sprang forward and dragged him to safety as Smiffy howled in pain. Another crew member had moved too slowly and was pitched over the side when an arrow caught him in the upper back. He entered the water with a splash and flailed weakly on the surface until he sank slowly under.

The ship continued, unable to turn back in the close confines of the stone walls. The oarsmen safe below decks increased their speed at a yell from the first mate. The Black Knight stayed on deck and took the helm as he was the only one with armour and a level of protection against the falling death from above. Looking up at the caves he saw the enemy archers firing as fast as they could. These were savages who lived amongst the cliffs and in the dark caves. The Black Knight had heard that they lived to attack passing ships and then lowered ropes from their caves to board the stricken ships. Any surviving crew were finished off, the vessel looted and then sunk. That wouldn't happen today, though.

Soon enough, the Dragon's Tooth passed beyond the caves and the whistling arrows. The deck looked like the back of a porcupine and the crew had to pull every arrow of the wood and stack them neatly for what lay ahead. Smiffy had been taken down below to the doctor and had the arrow pulled out of his leg, complaining loudly all the while.

Whooooosh! A fireball swept past the Black Knight's head and hit the main mast of the Dragon's Tooth. The mast caught fire as another ball of flame hit the side of the ship, knocking it sideways with the force. The flames licked up the mast and flickered up from over the side.

"Fire Eels!" yelled the Black Knight. "You men, get those buckets of water and douse the flames. Archers to the sides."

Men ran as they were bid and soon the mast fire had been put out. Another fireball soared overhead, missing the ship but bursting against the rock wall and illuminating the gorge in a flash. Another hit the ships wheel, making the helmsman jump back to avoid the flames. After a bucket of water had been thrown over it, the helmsman was able to steer the ship again, though the wood was still smoking.

The Black Knight went to the side of the ship and grabbed a bow from one of the archers who were trying to see a Fire Eel to shoot at. He strung an arrow and waited. Suddenly he saw one in the water, swimming under the ship. It was enormous, a gigantic snake that moved with incredible speed. Then it seemed to stop and moved to the surface, poking its head up and looking toward the Dragon's Tooth. The Black Knight could see that it was covered in red scales with a triangular head and a ridge of black spines running along its back. The creature opened its mouth, revealing a row of huge fangs and blasted a fireball at the ship.

The archers around the Black Knight yelled with fear and jumped out of the way as the fireball flew towards them. The Black Knight didn't move and instead aimed carefully and fired his arrow. It hissed straight toward the Fire Eel, passing the fireball in mid-air and slammed into the eels huge head, jerking it backwards and killing it instantly. The great red body vanished below the water. The fireball burst when it hit the Black Knight's chest, lifting him off his feet and throwing him across the deck.

"Is he dead?!" shouted the Captain, rushing forward.

"I'm fine," the Black Knight muttered, getting to his feet. His armour bore no damage. "Fire can't damage this," he said as he clanged a fist against his chest plate.

"I can't see any more Eels My Lord," Captain Courtney said, heaving a sigh of relief.

The ship continued, with the crew putting out the last of the fires on deck. One of the crew shouted with joy.

"I can see the end of the gorge ahead! We're nearly out!"

The crew cheered at this and the oarsmen went even faster. The Black Knight didn't cheer. He knew there was one more danger they hadn't seen yet.

Sure enough, before the crew even stopped cheering, the Dragon's Tooth lurched to one side as if it had hit a rock.

"Whirlpool!" On the starboard side of the ship a huge spinning mass of water had appeared out of nowhere. It spiralled into a seething centre and the Dragon's Tooth was being pulled toward it.

"Oarsmen, pull! Pull for your lives!" yelled the Captain.

"Throw anything heavy overboard," ordered the Black Knight.

The crew began to throw boxes, the spare anchor and anything else they could lay a hand to overboard in an attempt to lighten the ship. Still the whirlpool sucked them toward the centre. If the ship was pulled in it would be whisked underwater and never seen again, everyone on board consigned to a watery grave.

Inch by inch the Dragon's Tooth was drawn backwards towards the centre of the whirlpool. The crew were getting desperate by now.

"Should we throw His Lordships horse overboard?" whispered one crewman everyone called Podge due to his fondness for sticky buns and whatever else he could lay his hands on. Suddenly, Podge was lifted off the ground by the Black Knight.

"Try that, and you'll be going overboard after him," whispered the Black Knight.

Podge nodded, too scared to speak.

Suddenly, an idea came to the Black Knight. The ship only had to stay afloat for a while; these whirlpools came and went suddenly. He ran to the bow of the ship and uncovered the mighty harpoon crossbow which was used to hunt the massive Spindle fish near the Fair Isles.

The Black Knight rapidly cranked the thick silken rope back until it locked in place. He scooped up one of the 6-foot iron harpoons and loaded the weapon and then pointed it toward the rock wall of the gorge and fired. The huge harpoon shot out of the bow and embedded itself in the rock. The rope which attached the harpoon to the ship tightened as the ship was pulled backwards more but then it became taut.

The harpoon held and the Dragon's Tooth wasn't moving backwards anymore. They were saved!

Slowly, the whirlpool weakened and then vanished altogether. After the rope to the harpoon was cut, the Dragon's Tooth got underway again. They had survived the Black Gates and emerged into the Dark Seas and all the dangers they would soon face there.

Chapter 3

The Dragon's Tooth limped to the first port in the Dark Seas, Port Sandown. Repairs were needed to the fire damaged mast and the Black Knight had to get information on where Calico Jack's ship might be or which one of the many islands in the Dark Seas he was using as a base.

Once the ship was tied up beside a rickety dock, the Black Knight ordered Captain Courtney to get the mast repaired as fast as possible so they could leave this rat infested place and get back to the task at hand. He left the ship on Bolt and trotted along the quay to the market, his hand on his sword hilt. The greedy eyes of pirates, thieves and beggars that watched him lingered on the fine horse and that legendary armour but they knew who he was and no one was brave enough to go near the Black Knight much less attempt to steal anything from him.

The Black Knight reached the market and called out.

"Anyone who can tell me where the pirate called Calico Jack Rackham is now, come forward and you will have a bag of gold coins." He held up a small bag.

No one moved. Even though they were scared of the Black Knight, they were even more scared of Captain Rackham, or Calico Jack as he was known. He had picked up the nickname of 'Calico' for his love of fine clothes and, in particular, ones made from calico, a cotton like material, which was finer than the canvas usually worn by sailors.

Sighing, the Black Knight got off his horse, his boots slapping into the stone. Reaching the nearest market stall, he kicked the bench over, spilling rotten apples, green carrots and mouldy bread everywhere. The owner of the stall who had been hiding underneath found himself looking at the Black Knight towering over him.

"I don't even know who this Rackham is! I swear!" He whimpered.

The Black Knight didn't say anything but reached down, grabbed the man's filthy ankle and, with one hand, lifting him in the air so that he dangled upside down.

"Let me go, please, I don't know anything!"

Still holding him, the Black Knight walked to the dockside and held him over the water below. Both men could see a fin above the water and the body of the huge shark moving lazily just beneath the surface. The harbour attracted the hungry predators of the deep with the scraps and fish guts that were tossed into its waters.

"Alright, alright, I'll tell you! I heard Calico Jack's ship was at Skull Island. He's got a base there. That's all I know, he hasn't been to Sandown in months!"

The Black Knight lifted the man back from the water and dropped him on the dock with a bump. The man sat and rubbed his ankle and then exclaimed in surprise when the bag of gold clinked onto his lap. The Black Knight had turned to walk away when the man called out after him.

"There's something else My Lord." The Black Knight stopped and looked back. The man got to his feet and came close enough for the Black Knight to smell his fetid breath as he whispered.

"Blackbeard's back."

The man then turned on his heel and scampered back into the market, disappearing from view.

The Black Knight returned quickly to The Dragon's Tooth, thinking about what the man had said. Blackbeard had been gone from the Dark Seas for 10 years and it was rumoured he had been burnt to cinders by a dragon when he tried to steal the its gold. If he was alive and back in the Dark Seas then the Black Knight had to be careful. Blackbeard was the most vicious and terrifying pirate there had ever been and his ship, The Bonecrusher, had so many cannons that it could blast another ship to pieces in minutes. When ships captains saw it coming they didn't even try to fight, instead they surrendered instantly and hoped that Blackbeard was happy with what he could take from their hold. If he wasn't happy, everyone knew what he would do.

"Cast off and get underway," shouted Captain Courtney after the Black Knight nodded to him. The repairs to the ship had been hastily done, with fresh spars having been brought from the hold to replace the fire damaged ones. The mast would hold sails again.

The Dragon's Tooth edged out of Port Sandown under oar power and then hoisted its two great black sails once clear of the harbour. Everyone on board was glad to be away from Sandown, even though it was the last relatively safe port in the Dark Seas. They were heading for Skull Island, deep within the Dark Seas. The Black Knight had told the Captain about Blackbeard but ordered him not to tell the crew. Captain Hook was bad enough but if they knew Blackbeard was back it would terrify them.

The ship sailed all day, with a strong wind pushing The Dragon's Tooth along and the crew going about their jobs. These included getting some cannon practice and every few minutes a huge BOOM would sound and a plume of water would be thrown up by the cannon ball hurtling into the sea.

Other crew members were practicing their swordplay on deck and Podge yelped when someone poked him in the bum with the tip of a sword. Smiffy, limping around and complaining about his sore leg to anyone who would listen was ordered to paint over the scorch marks on the side of the ship that the Fire Eels had made. He was lowered down on a seat tied to a rope, with two sailors lowering or raising him as needed. The Black Knight stood in the bows and scanned the horizon, watching for any sign of ships. Pirate ships were notoriously fast and a constant lookout had to be kept.

"Aghhhhhhhhh!" A scream pierced the air and a judder ran through the ship as something heavy thumped into the port side. The crew rushed to the side and looked down. Smiffy was gone. All that remained the frayed end of the rope.

"What's going on?!" shouted the Black Knight.

"Not sure My Lord, the rope must have snapped on Smiffy. I can't see him in the water though." The Captain leaned over the side and looked back. He was about to order the ship to turn around to look for Smiffy when an enormous beast erupted from the sea like a green torpedo, heading straight for the captain, its jaws wide open and Smiffy's paintbrush stuck between two of the pointed white teeth that were as big as a man's foot. Just as those teeth were about to close on Courtney's head, the Black Knight reached forward, grabbed the back of his jacket and yanked him backward to safety. The terrible teeth snapped shut on thin air where the captains head had been and the great sea crocodile fell back into the sea.

"Don't lean over the sides of the ship! We're in croc territory," roared the Black Knight.

The sea crocodiles of the Dark Seas were just another danger to add to the list.

For three days the Dragon's Tooth continued across the Dark Seas, an unhappy ship. Smiffy's loss had affected the crew as, despite his bellyaching, Smiffy had been popular. On the second day a dense fog swept across the water and enveloped the ship, reducing visibility to the sides of the Dragon's Tooth and no further. In the middle of the dense white fog, the Dark Seas were completely silent.

After three long days and nights in the fog, the crew of the Dragon's Tooth were nearing breaking point. No one had sailed in conditions like this before and the Captain had no way of knowing what was ahead and if they were about to hit rocks, another ship or another sea crocodile.

"How do we know where we're going?" The Black Knight stood beside the Captain at the bows. The Captain was doing his stint on bow-watch and trying to spot any dangers ahead as the ship crept slowly forward in the light wind.

"I'm afraid we don't My Lord. Normally I would drop anchor and wait the fog out but the sea is just too deep for the amount of chain we have," The Captain scratched his short beard and went on, "My Lord, the crew…"

The Black Knight cut him off abruptly, "if any of the crew aren't happy Captain, they are welcome to leave the ship whenever they wish."

The Captain nodded jerkily "Of course my Lord, the crew will be fine."

Chapter 4

On the fourth day the fog lifted as soon as it had appeared and the empty seas were visible once more. The Captain called the whole crew to the main deck and bellowed.

"His Lordship has asked me to tell you that each of you will receive an extra bag of gold when we return home and an extra tot of rum tonight!"

The crew cheered at that and the Dragon's Tooth was a happier ship again.

Late in the afternoon, as the sun was beginning its descent toward the sea in the west, the mast top lookout called out "Sails dead ahead!" Even in armour, the Black Knight climbed the rigging to the crow's nest as fast as any of the crew and saw the white smudge in the distance that slowly sharpened into sails and then a ship as they drew closer.

"Ready for action! Run out the cannons! Crew, arm yourselves!" the Captain called from the deck below. The Dragon's Tooth's 18 cannons were run out, their barrels bristling along the side of the ship. The crew who weren't manning the cannon were passed weapons by the Second Mate, a Fair Isler nicknamed Hamfist for his massive hands.

Soon, everyone had a sword in their belt and the archers had quivers of arrows on their backs.

The Dragon's Tooth bore down on the ship, the crew eager for a fight after the terrors of the Black Gates and the attack by the sea crocodile. The Dragon's Tooth closed on the ship quickly. It was of a similar size to the Dragon's Tooth and looked as fast. It didn't have full sails out though, which confused the Captain – why would they let the Dragon's Tooth come so close, in the Dark Seas of all places, where pirates were rife and laws laughed at? As this thought crossed his mind, the sleek ship ahead put on full sail, the white sheets filling instantly with wind. The Dragon's Tooth was so close that the Black Knight could read the name on the transom of the other ship;

'Ranger'

He could also see the Skull and Crossbones fluttering at the mast.

"It's Rackham's ship!" he realised and swung out of the crow's nest, descending quickly to the deck. Other crew members had noticed the name by now and were craning their necks to see more of the infamous pirates ship. Everyone had heard tales of its speed and firepower and how Calico Jack had become the scourge of the Dark Seas ever since Blackbeard had vanished. Their excitement was tinged with dread; this would be a tough fight but they would be able to tell their children that they had fought Jack Rackham's men!

A boom sounded across the water from the other ship and, with a plume of smoke erupting from a rear gun, a cannonball hurtled towards the Dragon's Tooth.

"Everyone down!" thundered the Black Knight.

The cannonball was too high and tore a neat hole through the sails. The next shot would be on target, there was little doubt.

"Man the bow chaser, quickly now," yelled the Captain, "start firing at them."

Neither ship were able to bring their mighty broadside cannons to bear as the Dragon's Tooth was directly behind the Ranger, but each ship had smaller cannons at the front and rear which could still cause damage.

Before the cannon on Dragon's Tooth could start firing, another shot blasted away from the Ranger and the red hot cannonball slammed into the rigging of the Dragon's Tooth, snapping spars and bringing down the fore sail in the process. Podge and another crew man rushed forward to rig the sail again. The Dragon's Tooth lost some speed and began to fall back from the Ranger.

"Hit them you fools!" the Captains voice was hoarse as he yelled at the bow gunners who had started firing in response. If they could bring down a sail or, better yet, one of the masts of the enemy ship, then they would have a chance to board her and hopefully find the White Knight somewhere on board. The small bowchaser cannon wasn't powerful enough to hole the other ship however.

The bowchaser cannon of the Dragon's Tooth scored its first hit when a cannonball was sent whistling through the windows of the rear cabin of the Ranger, broken glass being punched inward. A loud cheer erupted from the crew.

"Hope you like that one Jacky!" Podge yelled.

Over the next few hours the two ships traded shots with minor damage being suffered by both. One of the crew, a skinny lad called Jim was left dangling upside down when a cannonball tore through the rigging he was standing on. Luckily his foot was caught in the rigging as he fell.

"Land Ahoy!" called the lookout from the crow's nest.

An island had been sighted ahead, with both ships closing on it as the day went on. The island wasn't large but it was dominated by a towering mountain in the middle and lush jungle at its base which then gave way to a white sand beach. The island was surrounded by smaller islands which formed a screen around the larger one.

"Is this Skull Island?" asked Hamfist, the Second Mate.

"No, you'll know Skull Island when you see it. This is just a normal island, probably full of savages or crocs, but nowhere we're interested in, that's for sure," the Captain replied.

Ahead, the Ranger seemed to be slowing down as it neared the smaller surrounding islands. A sail had been lowered!

"Why is he slowing?" queried the Black Knight. He sensed something wasn't quite right. Rackham's ship wasn't badly damaged and there was no need to drop sails if they wanted to vanish into the cluster of islands. The cannons had long since stopped firing as they were unable to seriously damage the other ship. The Dragon's Tooth closed on the Ranger and by the time it was near enough to easily make out the figures on the enemy ships deck. The Ranger was gliding past a steep sided rocky island on its starboard side. The Skull and Crossbones flapped in the wind as the tall man with a wide black hat and deep red coat stepped to the back of the forecastle. It was Calico Jack himself!

The Black Knight was standing in the bow of the Dragon's Tooth and both men stared at each other. Captain

Rackham was as tall as the Black Knight and had a long sword at his hip. He raised an arm in greeting at the pursuing ship. The Black Knight did not wave back. Laughing now, Captain Rackham raised his hat and then swept it before him, bowing as he did so and then straightened and shouted, "Good luck little knight!" His shark like grin was visible even from a distance.

With that, the Ranger put on full sails and then jumped forward as its oars slid out and began rowing furiously. Amongst islands like this, using oars was an insane tactic. If an oar snagged on a rock it would kill the oarsman easily and foul the other rowers as well.

The Ranger moved past the rock on the starboard side and the Black Knight suddenly knew something was very deeply wrong.

Chapter 5

"Turn around!!!" he yelled. It was too late. The Dragon's Tooth passed the huge rocky island as well. Beside it lay a large bay which had been hidden from view by the rocky island. Out of that bay a gargantuan ship emerged, thrusting forward under oar power and heading straight for the Dragon's Tooth. The ship was painted black with pitch, with black sails and had a pointed ram that lay half underwater at the bow. The ship was twice as big as the Dragon's Tooth and, at the top of its mast there flew a black flag with a broken bone displayed on it in white. It was the Bonecrusher, Blackbeard's ship!

Two huge cannons protruded from the bow, each as big as any of The Dragon's Tooth's main guns. In twin blasts of fire and smoke they both fired at the same time, the balls slamming into the side of the Dragon's Tooth and throwing the crew to the deck with the impact. The holes in Dragon's Tooth were still above the waterline thankfully. That didn't matter too much however as the black ship kept coming without a check and smashed into the side of the Dragon's Tooth, the ram slamming deeply into her at the water line.

This time the whole ship lurched, carried sideways by the impact. The Black Knight leapt for a rope to stop him being thrown overboard as some of the crew had been. He saw Podge's head bobbing in the water as he gasped and spat water from his mouth.

The Bonecrusher's oars stopped and both ships, locked together, stopped moving. Without the ram of the Bonecrusher holding it up, the Dragon's Tooth would already have sunk. Only the sheer size of the Bonecrusher prevented the stricken Dragon's Tooth from dragging it under.

Suddenly, a horrible screaming began from the black ship above. Figures swarmed to the edge of the Bonecrusher and some jumped the distance between the ships, others swung across on ropes. All had swords or axes and all were screaming as they came.

Blackbeard's crew! Above them, still on Bonecrusher, the Black Knight could see Captain Blackbeard standing in the bows.

His hands were on his hips and his head was thrown back as he laughed an evil laugh. He was an enormous man, taller that the Black Knight, with a huge bushy black beard that reached almost to his belt. On each hip he had a sword and across his chest were a selection of knives and small axes. In each hand he held what looked like cannonballs, though the Black Knight couldn't be sure before the first of the Bonecrusher's crew reached him and what was left of his crew. Half had been thrown overboard when the ship was hit. Drawing his sword, the Black Knight charged, followed by his crew who roared their anger at the loss of their ship. The first of Blackbeard's crew he reached was a hulking mountain of a man with a huge battle-axe that he swung in an arc towards the Black Knight.

The axe was stopped in mid-air by the Black Knight's sword, which swept it aside. The Black Knight then butted his helmet into the man's grimy face, making him stagger back, blood gushing from his broken nose. The Black Knight's sword flashed down and the man fell to the deck. The Black Knight charged on into the middle of the enemy crew, sweeping his sword left and right, supported by Captain Courtney on his right hand side and the remaining crew. Each man of the Dragon's Tooth fought like a demon for they knew they fought for their lives. At the sound of a blaring horn high up on Bonecrusher's deck, the pirate crew suddenly backed away, breathing hard and leaving dead crew mates in their wake. They were smiling though. The Black Knight, his bloody sword still held aloft, looked up and saw that Blackbeard had stepped forward to the edge of his ship. The objects in his hands were now giving off wisps of smoke. Blackbeard, grinning hugely, lifted one arm after the other and hurled the objects towards the Black Knight and his crew.

"Bombs!" Turning, the Black Knight yelled at his crew "Run!"

Both bombs exploded at the same time in a flash of flame and smoke, shredding the deck of the Dragon's Tooth and lifting the remaining crew into the air as if they weighed nothing. Some were thrown into the sea, some further along the deck, left to lie like torn dolls. Captain Courtney had leapt in front of the Black Knight when the bombs hit the deck taking the brunt of the blast that would have hit his master. The bravery of the Captain and the Black Knight's armour saved his life but did not stop him being hurled overboard into the sea, unconscious from the force of the blast. The Black Knight sank swiftly to the sandy seabed and lay there unmoving. His ship followed the Black Knight quickly underwater after the Bonecrusher pulled backward under oar power again, releasing its ram from the bowels of the Dragon's Tooth in a splintering of timbers. The broken ship settled gently on the seabed. The crew of the Dragon's Tooth who were still in the water from the initial ramming by the Bonecrusher were picked off one by one by pirate archers. Within fifteen minutes of the sinking of the Dragon's Tooth, all were gone.

The Black Knight did not see the Bonecrusher sailing away above him. He didn't hear Blackbeard's crew cheering. He couldn't even feel the cold water of the Dark Seas. He definitely didn't feel the hands that lifted him from the seabed, his helmet being removed and the mouth that gave him the kiss of life. He didn't see the graceful bodies beside him as they swam him to shore, their large fins pumping them onward.

When the mermaids reached the sandy beach they stopped in the shallows and pushed the Black Knight onto the sand, though the sea still lapped against his armour. They had slipped his sword back into its scabbard and laid his helmet close at hand. The red-haired mermaid turned to her sister.

"Should we just leave him here? Who is he?"

Her older sister, who always seemed to know what to do at any given moment and could always find the tastiest fish and fattest lobsters smiled and turned to her sister.

"He's no pirate for a start. Look at that armour – it has magic of some kind in it. No, this isn't a bad man. A hard man, yes, but not a bad man."

31

"Ok, but do we just leave him? What if the Tiger Crabs find him before he wakes?!" The red-haired mermaids face creased with worry.

"We'll wait until he wakes up and then I'd say he's more than capable of taking care of himself," the dark haired older sister assured her.

The mermaids settled down to wait in the shallows, their long tails spread out on the sand under the water and each enjoying the sun. Thankfully none of the hideous Tiger Crabs that infested the island ventured out of their nests at the top of the beach.

The Black Knight suddenly began to cough violently and vomited seawater onto the golden sand. After a moment he sat up and saw two tail fins dipping into the sea. He was alone.

'Where am I' he thought, standing and looking along the empty beach. Then it all came flooding back. Rackham. Blackbeard. His ship! Anger threatened to engulf the Black Knight. So many good men had died. He didn't even know why Rackham had kidnapped the White Knight or why he had teamed up with Blackbeard. Those two should be sworn enemies.

The Black Knight picked up his helmet and held it whilst his short dark hair began to dry in the sun. The scar that ran from his right temple down to his jaw gave the impression of cruelty, which was enhanced by the cold green eyes that stared at the world and found it wanting. It was the wide mouth that saved the face and softened the otherwise harsh lines. The laughter lines surrounding it and the upturned sides revealed a glimpse of the man behind the piercing eyes.

Chapter 6

The Black Knight began walking along the beach, knowing that he had to find some way off this island. There must be some kind of port or harbour where he could buy a ship with the gold he still had. If they refused, well, he would have to take a ship with the sword he still had.

The island was small and it didn't take long to walk all the way around it and then to the top of the hill in the centre. At that modest height, the Black Knight could see that he was on one of the smaller islands in the cluster.

The biggest island was a mile away and had to be the best opportunity to get a boat. But how to get there?! The Black Knight began to walk back down to the beach, through the trees that covered the small island. He was so deep in thought that he didn't notice the scuttling noises coming from the undergrowth around him. He did notice the scraping noise from the branches of the tree above him however and, looking up, saw the armoured body falling toward him, two fearsome claws outstretched. The Black Knight threw himself backward, dropping his helmet and drawing his sword as he did so. The two claws, which would have closed on the Black Knight's shoulders, hit the sword instead, clamping onto it like two vices, almost wresting it from his grip. The square body of the Tiger Crab crashed into the Black Knight, throwing him to the ground with the crab on top of him, its claws still gripping the sword. The crab was the size of a large dog and twice as heavy. Its striped red armour was serrated at the edges and pockmarked with limpets. The Black Knight could feel the 6 pointed legs rattling against his armour, the sharp spikes feeling for a weak spot to stab him. With a stab like a knife, the Black Knight felt one of the spiked legs jab into his upper thigh. Out of the corner of his eye, the Black Knight saw another Tiger Crab scuttle into view through the undergrowth. Two of these beasts would be the end of him. With a supreme effort, the Black Knight took one hand off the sword which was holding the huge claws at bay and scrabbled for his dagger. His fingers closed on the black leather handle and, with a thrust, the Black Knight drove the dagger into the weaker armour on the crabs belly. Instantly the crab loosened the sword and rolled off the Black Knight, clawing at its belly. The Black Knight leapt to his feet just in time to avoid the rush of the second crab. His sword flickered out and the second crab lost one of its claws and decided that this prey wasn't worth the risk.

Another thrust of the blade into the dying Tiger Crab finished it off and the forest was quiet once more. Looking down, the Black Knight breathed a sigh of relief when he saw that the wound to his thigh wasn't deep. After binding it with a strip torn from his shirt, he gathered up his helmet and jammed it on his head.

Carrying the crab claw he had removed from his attacker, the Black Knight reached the beach and almost laughed at what he saw. A small sailing dinghy had been pushed up on the sand. Two heads, one red haired and the other dark brown, bobbed in the sea just offshore.

'That's who saved me! Mermaids! Of course.!' The Black Knight realised. He raised a hand to thank them for saving his life twice now and watched as they waved back and dived, their glistening tails rising above the water before vanishing beneath it.

The Black Knight made a small fire on the beach and replenished his strength with the crab meat before pushing the dinghy out over the hot sand and jumping aboard. Time to see what was on the big island.

The dirty white sail rose with a squeak and clatter as the Black Knight pulled it up. It then filled with a snap, pulling the boom out to port and getting the small craft moving through the water towards the distant island. The Black Knight took stock of the situation; he had no ship big enough to reach Skull Island. He had no crew. He had no fresh water, though at least he had the remains of the crab claw he had cooked. Of weaponry, he had his sword and dagger at least, and the armour of course, which had saved his skin more times than he could remember. If he couldn't find a ship on this island, what could he do though? Was he destined to die on a deserted island, or be picked off by local savages or local beasts?

As the island drew closer, the Black Knight's dinghy moved into the shadow cast by the mountain that rose from its centre. The sun was going down and darkness would be on him soon. Not the best time to land on unknown shores. Bumbling about in the dark jungle would make it very easy for Tiger Crabs or who knows what else to catch him unawares. In the swiftly fading light, the Black Knight thought he could see wisps of smoke at the mountains peak, but the breeze whipped them away before he could be sure.

When the bow of the dinghy crunched on the white sand of the island dusk had fallen and the dense jungle at the top of the beach was dark and unbroken as far as the eye could see.

Rather than risk a night on the beach, vulnerable to easy attack, the Black Knight pushed the dinghy offshore a short distance and threw the small anchor overboard, checking the rope to make sure it had caught on the sandy bottom. Satisfied, the Black Knight made himself as comfortable as possible in the cramped confines of the dinghy, took off his helmet and finished off the last of the crab before falling asleep.

Chapter 7

"Aghhhhhhhhhhhh," a high-pitched scream woke him with a start. The Black Knight sat upright, scrabbling for his helmet. The sun was just about to peak over the horizon to the east and three figures came into view on the sandy beach, the first having burst out of the jungle and running down to the firmer sand near the water before turning in the Black Knight's direction.

The two other figures that followed were side by side and carrying what looked like spears. One cocked his arm back and hurled a spear, narrowly missing the running man but bringing another terrified scream from him.

Recognition jolted the Black Knight. He knew that voice from the Dragon's Tooth! It was Podge, who he had last seen in the water after the Bonecrusher rammed the ship. He had made it ashore after all.

The Black Knight hauled in the anchor and fitted the oars into the rowlocks. Pulling furiously, the dingy soon crunched onto the sand. The Black Knight leapt into the shallows, drawing his sword as he did so. Podge was red in the face, his arms pumping, but a look of shocked relief on his podgy features when he saw the Black Knight. The two pursuers had gained on him and the man that had thrown the spear had plucked it out of the sand as he ran. Podge reached the Black Knight and collapsed on the sand behind him, too winded to even speak.

The two pursuers came on, spears held above their heads. They were both small men but powerfully built, with ridged muscle on their bare chests. Each had whorls of intricate black tattoos covering every inch of exposed skin, which was quite a lot, given that the only clothing they wore was a loincloth. Their heads had been plucked of all hair and more tattoos covered their scalps. Their mouths were open with their panting after the chase and the Black Knight could see the row of sharpened teeth. These were the Painted People, the Black Knight realised, cursing his luck for landing on this island. They lived on some of the islands in the Black Seas and were named for their love of tattooing their whole bodies with the stories of their people. They were a warlike bunch, with each clan constantly fighting others. Any outsiders that landed on their shores had a short life expectancy.

One of the Painted People was slightly ahead of the other and reached the Black Knight first, doing a slight jump in the air and thrusting with his spear towards the Black Knight's chest. The great sword swept the spear aside and the Black Knight turned his shoulder to let the man crash into it. The impact sent the smaller man spinning off to the side, but he rolled nimbly and came to his feet clutching a wickedly curved dagger that had been tucked into the loin cloth. The second attacker didn't go for the overhead lunge but dropped his spear to waist height and tried to use his momentum to break through the Black Knight's defence.

The Black Knight knocked the tip of the spear to one side, stepped to the other side and let the Painted Man come on, slamming the pommel of his sword into the top of the man's head. The man fell to the sand unconscious. The other man howled and hurled himself at the Black Knight, his dagger held out and aiming for the knight's throat. The Black Knight whirled to face him and the long sword swept up. The Painted Man's dagger fell to the sand, the hand still clutching it. The islander did not stop however and kept coming at the Black Knight, barely registering the loss of his hand. This time the sword flickered out again and slid into the man's chest, making him stop in his tracks, his eyes glazing immediately. The Black Knight withdrew his sword and the dead man fell to the sand.

"Thank you My Lord! Thank you, thank you," gasped Podge, who still lay huddled on the sand.

After cleaning his sword, the Black Knight sheathed it and helped Podge to his feet.

"Were these the only two or did you see more?" he enquired. An attack by a clan of the Painted People could only end badly.

"I just saw these two My Lord. I swam ashore…I nearly drowned…got to the beach…" Podge was stumbling over the words, clearly exhausted by everything that had happened since the previous day.

"Did you see a village, a port, anything useful?" cut in the Black Knight.

"Sorry. Once I got to shore I hid in the jungle until I heard something in the bushes and ran. I don't think I stopped all night My Lord! Then, when light broke, these devils saw me." He gestured to the two attackers, one of whom was starting to wake up. The Black Knight snatched Podge's sweaty bandanna from his head and neatly bound the Painted Man's hands behind his back before he woke fully. The clansman's eyes suddenly popped open and he began to buck and struggle against his bonds, snapping his sharp teeth at the Black Knight and Podge, who hurried to stand behind him again.

"Savage little guy isn't he," muttered the Black Knight, drawing his dagger and stepping forward. The Painted Man quietened when he saw the armoured knight approaching. "Let's hope you speak some of my language, for your sake."

A short time later the Black Knight and Podge, who was now armed with a spear, entered the jungle, heading for the mountain. The Painted Man had understood and proved surprisingly helpful after the Black Knight had explained the man's options; answer some simple questions and live. Don't, and die. As the two men entered the jungle the Painted Man was snoring softly into the sand, having been re-introduced to the swords pommel. What he had told the Black Knight may prove the answer to their predicament and meant that they had to head inland, towards the mountain. It could just as easily lead to their deaths if the Black Knight's hunch was wrong.

"Begging pardon My Lord, but why didn't you kill that islander fella?" queried Podge, glancing behind the two as they walked up the beach toward the looming jungle.

"I only kill who I have to kill, Podge," the green eyes turned toward the smaller man "and that does not include a bound captive."

Podge's face went redder than it had already been and he nodded jerkily.

The gloom of the jungle closed around the two men. After the bright early morning sunshine of the open beach, the jungle was oppressive. The Black Knight knew he was taking an enormous risk but, if the Painted Man had been telling the truth, this was the only way off the island and the only chance he had to reach his brother and rescue him from Rackham or Blackbeard.

Podge was panting again and wiping beads of sweat from his forehead as the pair trudged through the thick jungle, with the Black Knight slashing branches out of the way to create a path. Even though his armour was incredibly light, it wasn't just Podge who found the going tough. High above them, the sun was trying and failing to get through the heavy canopy of leaves. Its heat, however, still got through and the humidity at ground level was stifling. After two hours of climbing, Podge dropped to his knees.

"My Lord, can I rest? Do we have any water?!" He croaked through parched lips.

"We keep going Podge. The Painted Man said there was a clearing half-way up the volcano," replied the Black Knight.

Podge dropped to all fours, his face now puce and his breath coming in heaving gulps, "I'm sorry My Lord, I don't think I can get up."

Sighing, the Black Knight lifted the fat man bodily onto his shoulder and set off again through the trees, climbing again.

After another hour the two emerged into an opening in the trees and into bright sunshine.

Chapter 8

The grass grew waist high around a shimmering pool of water about 10 feet across. At one patch beside the pool the grass had been worn down to the bare soil, but strangely there was no path leading from the treeline to the pool. Beyond the area of grass that encircled the pool the rest of the glade was bare soil, on which only small shoots of new growth were beginning to show. The glade had been enlarged by something that was able to uproot whole trees and carry them away. The area still showed the deep scars where mighty trees had once stood. The Painted Man hadn't been lying at least, the Black Knight thought.

He laid the now sleeping Podge down on the grass and walked to the deep blue pool. Taking his helmet off, he scooped up water and drank deeply before filling the helmet again and returning to Podge, who was stirring. He gulped the water frantically without opening his eyes. The Black Knight slipped the helmet back on and savoured the cool metal against his scalp.

Above the glade a fountain of smoke rose from the summit of the volcano and a deep rumbling ran through the earth beneath the men.

"The volcanos about to blow My Lord! We need to run!" squeaked Podge, struggling to get to his feet.

The Black Knight restrained the panicking man with a hand on his shoulder "Stop. The last thing you should do is run. I need you to walk slowly to the trees and hide out of sight. It's not the volcano." With that, Podge was pushed gently towards tree line whilst his master moved to the bare patch beside the pool, making himself easily visible. Looking over his shoulder as he entered the shade of the trees, Podge saw the Black Knight draw his sword, place its point in the ground and rest both hands on the pommel.

From the peak of the volcano came an almighty whoosh and a jet of flame shot into the air, incinerating a passing bird in a puff of burnt feathers. After the gout of flame, a plume of grey smoke billowed from the peak.

"He was wrong," whispered Podge "the volcano is erupting!" He wished he'd run but his legs still felt like rubber.

The ground trembled and the from the mountain shot a black mass, straight into the air. When it began to lose speed, two enormous wings unfolded from the bullet shaped body and began to beat. The jet black body was covered in triangular scales that shone in the sunlight. The creature looked to be the same size as The Dragon's Tooth and when the wings stretched to their full extent they could have covered a house. The wings were tipped with talons, each as long as Podge stood tall. The creatures head sat at the end of a graceful neck and was the size of a carriage. The huge mouth was open as it soared skyward, revealing twin rows of sharp white teeth. Smoke streamed from the nostrils as the creature stopped climbing and seemed to stop in mid-air, holdings its position with sweeps of its wings, the force of which bent the grass in the glade many feet below.

Podge's mouth fell open. A dragon! An actual dragon! He would have rather it had been the volcano erupting. At least then he might have had a chance at survival. With a dragon, everyone knew there was no defeating it, even if you did have magic armour like the Black Knight. A dragon's fire could melt steel, it claws rip through stone and no known weapon could harm it. Old Bobbers at the castle used to tell tall tales that a Leviathans poison could get through the scales of a dragon. Podge cowered behind the trunk and waited for the dragon to decide who he wanted to eat first.

The great wings of the beast tucked into the body and the dragon plummeted toward the Black Knight like a stone. When it was 20 feet from the ground a tongue of flame shot from its mouth, scorching a path on the soil toward the lone figure. The Black Knight still hadn't moved and Podge was about to scream at him to run but didn't want the dragon knowing where he was hiding.

The dragon's feet touched the ground and it began skidding towards the Black Knight, flame still belching from its open mouth and a mound of soil being pushed before its claws. Just when the fire was about to engulf the knight, the flames vanished, to be replaced by a plume of smoke, which enveloped both the Black Knight and the dragon. Only the dragons tail, with its wicked arrow point, protruded from the smoke, sweeping from side to side.

Podge gathered his courage and was about to make a break for it when a breeze began to shift the white cloud. "What on earth." He gasped. There, in the middle of the glade, the Black Knight still stood. The dragon stood beside him but it had lowered its head as if to talk to the Black Knight. Wait, they were talking! For the second time in two minutes, Podge's mouth fell open.

"That was quite the appearance you made, Draco." The Black Knight thrust his sword into the ground and stepped forward, hiding his relief that his hunch had been right. Bowing respectfully, he straightened and smiled. "But it didn't work."

Draco The Hungry chuckled, a noise that sounded like wood under the saw and bowed its head to The Black Knight. "I was sure you were going to run." Its leathery lips broke into a wide grin that revealed gleaming fangs. "Your little friend amongst the trees did well to stay where he was." Again came the noise of sawing wood.

The Black Knight was desperate to get down to business but one does not rush a dragon, even if he's your friend.

"I didn't know you were in the Dark Seas, Draco. Last time I saw you was in the Far North." The Black Knight could well remember the battles he had fought in alongside Draco and his tribe against the Firewing dragons of the Northern Isles. It had been his idea to use Leviathan-poison-tipped harpoons. He shook aside the memory.

Containing his impatience, the Black Knight made the formal conversation that dragon etiquette requires. When they aren't burning villages and eating the population, dragons can be surprisingly stuffy about manners.

Eventually, Draco rumbled "Now, my friend, tell me the reason for your visit."

The Black Knight cleared his throat before beginning,

"My brother was taken by pirates. You won't know them but in human circles they are widely feared. I don't know how they managed to get him, but it must have been near his castle. As you know, it's near the entrance to the Black Gates."

Draco nodded, saying nothing. The Black Knight continued,

"He got me a message though and I set out immediately and set sail for the Dark Seas. In Port Sandown I found out that one of the pirates had been using Skull Island as a base."

Draco nodded again and rumbled, "You must know this is a trap to lure you to them? There is no other explanation as to why they did not simply kill your brother when they caught him."

The Black Knight had come to a similar conclusion. There was no other logical explanation behind all of this. The pirates wanted the brothers in the same place to finish them off once and for all. Then Blackbeard, Rackham and all the other scum could pour out of the Black Gates and prey on the soft targets of merchant vessels and the ports that currently enjoyed the protection of the castles of the knights.

Taking a deep breath, the Black Knight made his request "Will you fly me to Skull Island, Draco?" Its long been true that dragons don't like to involve themselves in the petty squabbles of man, seeing them as nothing more than a tasty appetiser. When you're a 1500-year-old near-invincible dragon, this viewpoint does make some sense.

Draco snorted in surprise, twin puffs of smoke coming out of his nostrils and his teeth baring in anger. To ask Draco The Hungry, chief of the Bloodflame dragons of Easterly, to carry a human like a common horse, was unheard of. In the battles against the Firewings, the Black Knight had ridden very junior dragons who were no more than 150 years old, and that was bad enough. At least they weren't much larger than horses.

Seeing the anger building in the great beast, the Black Knight quietly said, "Remember Ironclaw Pass."

Instantly Draco deflated, his anger gone. In the terrible battle that had ended the war in the Far North, the Black Knight had saved Draco's like by hurling the harpoon tipped with Leviathan poison. It had struck the enormous leader of the Firewing dragons who had been about to swoop down on an unsuspecting Draco flying beneath him. The Firewing chief had plunged into the ice below and vanished.

The other Firewings, still belching flame and fighting claw to claw with the Bloodflames, had seen their leader fall and fled.

"Very well, Knight. A debt is owed."

The Black Knight nodded in thanks. "Could you also bring my servant, who is still hiding in the trees?" Seeing the great dragon begin to swell in anger again, the Black Knight added quickly "Carry him in your claws if you must!"

Chapter 9

A short time later, when Podge had been dragged into the clearing by the Black Knight, the three prepared to leave the circle of the dragons watering hole. Draco had soared in to the air, leaving the men on the ground. They watched as he reached the summit of the volcano and disappeared inside.

"Has he abandoned us, My Lord?" queried Podge.

"You never really know with dragons," the Black Knight replied, taking the time to sharpen his longsword with a whetstone.

A short time later, Draco burst out of the volcano again and returned to the glade, landing with enough force to make Podge stumble. In one of his huge claws Draco carried what looked like a mass of wood and metal.

"Here, this may be of use to you in the fight to come," rumbled the dragon, dropping the tumble of weaponry near the Black Knight. This was clearly what some of Draco's victims had been holding when they had been lifted in the curved claws. Some of the weapons were burnt and twisted by the heat of the dragons flame so that they were unrecognisable. Others had been snapped in two by Draco's vice like talons when he lifted them. There were some usable weapons though they were a motley assortment of battle-axes that had seen better days and swords with rusted or nicked blades.

However, what was this? The Black Knight exclaimed in surprise when he saw it.

Lifting it by the polished wooden stock, The Black Knight held the beautiful and deadly weapon before him.

"Where did you find this, Draco?" He exclaimed.

Draco chuckled that wood saw chuckle as he heard the delight in the knight's voice. "I have no idea my friend, it looks like a toy to me!"

"This is no toy! It's a repeating crossbow. I've only heard stories about them."

The crossbow was slightly larger than a normal one, with a wooden stock and foregrip, on top of which ran an iron flight groove that led to the bow limbs. Unlike a normal crossbow, where the flight groove ran to the bow limbs and cocking stirrup, there lay a cylindrical barrel. Under the grip and behind the barrel was a cocking handle that, when pushed forward, loaded a bolt and cocked the waxed silk string behind it. When it fired using a small trigger beneath the stock, the handle could be cocked again, loading and firing another bolt in two seconds. All eight bolts could be fired within 10 seconds. It placed devastating firepower in one man's hands.

"My Lord!" shrilled Podge, "look at this." He held up a thick leather belt festooned with bolts.

The Black Knight nodded. "You take that Podge, and find yourself a decent axe."

Once ready, the two men faced the waiting dragon. Podge had found a blackened iron axe with a wooden handle and leather grip that he had strapped to his back. He had also found several spherical bombs and a length of fuse cord which he had stuffed into a bloodstained leather satchel. The Black Knight had similarly slung the repeating crossbow over his shoulder and added a quiver of iron bolts to his belt. Draco lowered a wing so that the talons brushed the earth and the Black Knight hopped lightly onto the beast, scrambling up to the spiny ridge behind Draco's head and settling himself. When Podge tried to follow, the Black Knight stopped him.

"Sorry Podge, Draco won't allow you to ride upon his back. I'm afraid you'll be going a different way."

Before poor Podge could utter a complaint, the great dragon reared up on its hind legs and scooped the portly sailor up in a foreclaw, holding him gently enough. Then the powerful legs squatted and, with an explosive surge, thrust the dragon into the air, the great wings unfolding at the same time and beginning to beat majestically, pulling it skyward. Podge's shriek of terror could barely be heard above the roar of the wind as Draco surged into the blue sky, leaving the island far below. The Black Knight wanted to shout with joy; this was how to travel! Podge was still shouting, but not with joy.

Draco levelled off and settled into a steady speed that brought the Black Knight and Podge toward Skull Island at incredible pace. The sea far below shone in the suns light and islands were dotted like crumbs across the Dark Seas. It didn't seem like much time had passed before the Black Knight sat upright in his perch on Draco's back. There it was! Ahead and far below, the unmistakable shape of a large skull shaped island was coming into view. The island had been a volcano eons before but a series of eruptions had left the volcano dormant and had blown three gaping holes in the landscape. Two sat to the north of the island and gave the appearance of eye sockets. The other was to the south and gaped like a mouth open in a silent scream. Each of the craters had filled with water, forming large crater lakes. It was from these craters that the island got its name.

The Black Knight shuffled forward on the dragon's neck, clinging to the red spines that were three feet long and led to the back of Draco's head. "can you put us down on that nearest beach?"

The Black Knight didn't want to alert the pirates on the island that they had arrived and he knew that Draco would refuse to get involved in the fight. That wasn't the worst thing as dragon fire is somewhat indiscriminate and the White Knight could easily get caught in the searing flames. From this high up, the Black Knight would see the fortress on the north side of the island, sitting between the two 'eyes' of the skull. A cluster of shanty huts clustered around its rough-hewn block walls and was as close as Skull Island seemed to have to any permanent town.

There were burnt out or abandoned huts, houses and even the remains of an ancient church scattered around the rest of the island. Perhaps Skull Island had once been a hospitable place, with a port, a church and happy islanders. Now, it was just a pirate base which housed the two most dangerous pirates in the known world.

Draco suddenly tucked his wings in to his body and plunged toward the deep waters below. A piercing shriek rose from where Podge remained ensconced in Draco's claw and continued until Draco levelled off just above the gentle waves that ran in marching rows towards the white sands of

Skull Island. When he reached the beach, the dragon tipped his body skyward, spread wings and slammed his hind claws into the soft sand, stopping almost immediately. As he did so, Draco released Podge, who was thrown headlong, ploughing a groove in the sand with his face. He raised his face and snorted sand from both nostrils.

"Praise be, we're on land again!" he rejoiced.

The Black Knight leapt from Draco's back, his boots sinking into the sand. Turning to the dragon, who had lowered its great head, the Black Knight bowed and received a bow from Draco in return. Without a further word, Draco turned on his heel, faced out towards the sea and sprang into the air, the backdraft from his wings sending a cloud of sand flying into the faces of the two men on the beach. Within seconds the mighty dragon was a speck in the sky.

"Thank goodness he's gone My Lord," spluttered Podge, spitting sand from his mouth. "He gave me the willies."

The Black Knight chuckled and clapped Podge on the shoulder. "Let's get moving; I want to be at the fortress by nightfall."

Chapter 10

The sun was beginning to slip toward the sea in the west as the two entered the trees, which were thankfully not as dense as on the last island. They began to make their way north, to rescue the White Knight, or die trying.

The going was easy and the island was mostly flat so the sun had just dipped below the horizon when the two reached the outskirts of the pirate town that surrounded the fortress. The Black Knight and Podge stopped just inside the treeline and about 100 feet from the first of the shanty huts near the fortress walls. Even from that distance they could smell the open sewers and rotting food that pirates had simply thrown on the ground. Figures staggered from amongst the huts and in and out of the open gates of the fortress, which hung askew from their brackets. Two torches had been lit and placed in brackets either side of the gates so that long shadows were thrown beyond the huts.

"Lazy devils couldn't even fix their own gates," muttered the Black Knight.

Beyond the gates, the fortress itself was a simple affair. The high block wall surrounded a cluster of wooden buildings in the courtyard with a fortified stone building in the centre. This would be the headquarters of Blackbeard and Rackham. As dusk advanced, the windows began to light up and the sound of music and laughter carried to the treeline. From the dirt road that led to the harbour came the sound of hooves and a large carriage came into view drawn by four huge black horses. The only people on the island who could be inside that carriage were the pirate captains. The White Knight would surely be locked somewhere inside the fortress. It was time to end this and deal with Blackbeard and Rackham once and for all.

From behind him the Black Knight heard a stifled gasp from Podge and turned quickly. Podge was holding both hands over his mouth to stop from screaming. In the failing light the Black Knight could see the ground moving by Podge's boots. No, that didn't make sense. Peering closer he saw that the ground wasn't moving! It was the movement of something. Something with scales that caught the light of the distant torches. A snake! And an enormous one at that. The serpent began to loop itself around Podge's legs, bringing another gasp of terror from the man. Coil after coil encircled his legs and he would have fallen but for a tree directly behind him. The Black Knight knew that after the snake had imprisoned its victim in its coils then it could start to squeeze and that would be the end of its victim.

"It's a constrictor Podge. It can't poison you," he whispered. This was a dangerous moment – if the snake was disturbed as it coiled around the man then it could lash out and deliver a horrific bite. Whilst the Choker Snake didn't use poison on its victims, it still had fangs like knives and the bite alone could still kill through blood loss or infection. Podge's eyes rolled back in his head as the snake continued, eventually reaching his chest. Then the vile triangular head bobbed up and the evil eyes seemed to stare into Podge's. Now was the time.

With one swift movement, the Black Knight drew his sword and lunged. If the snake hadn't been coiled entirely around Podge it might have been fast enough to react and strike at the Black Knight. The sword flashed and neatly decapitated the Choker Snake, the head falling to the ground and bouncing away. Like fat coils of rope, the snakes body fell away from Podge and he was able to suck in a deep breath.

"I think I've decided to become a farmer if I survive this My Lord!"

"Survive tonight and you can do just that," replied the Black Knight, turning back to the fortress. He needed to know how many men were inside that fortress and if the White Knight was there, and where he was being held inside the fortress. But how?

Just then, luck intervened in the shape of a pirate walking toward the treeline. Unlike his mates, this one seemed to want some privacy as he went to the toilet and had chosen the patch of forest where the Black Knight and Podge hid. Motioning Podge to stand out of sight, the Black Knight flattened himself against a tree trunk and waited. When the unsuspecting pirate entered the treeline, all he felt was an armoured glove clamp over his mouth and a powerful arm slip around his neck.

"Don't move and you might live," whispered a voice in his ear.

Podge hurried from his hiding place and quickly bound the pirates hands and feet with liana that he cut from a nearby tree and stuffed one of the pirates stinking socks into his mouth.

The Black Knight removed his dagger from its scabbard and idly played with it as the terrified pirate was hauled to a sitting position against a tree.

"I have some questions. You're going to answer them."

The Black Knight had barely spoken above a whisper but his tone made it clear to the pirate that he absolutely was going to tell this tall knight whatever he wanted to know.

Chapter 11

A short time later the pirate lay motionless in the soft undergrowth of the forest after the Black Knight had ended their conversation by slamming the hilt of the dagger into the side of his head. He wouldn't wake until the coming fight was long done. The pirate had spilled all the information he could, tripping over his words to keep the Black Knight's dagger from coming any nearer his face. Blackbeard and Rackham were indeed in the fortress. Blackbeard had just arrived and had been met at the harbour by Rackham in his carriage. The two captains had then returned to the fortress to celebrate the destruction of the Black Knight and plan the execution of the White Knight, who was being held in the topmost tower of the ancient fortress. The Black Knight had hissed in annoyance when he found out that the pirates had been well aware that his brother had sent the message via eagle messenger.

Beckoning Podge to crouch beside him, the Black Knight laid out the plan of attack. As he listened, Podge grew paler and was thankful for the darkness that hid his shaking hands. They had the element of surprise and the pirates thought them dead, but there were still many pirates in that pale stone fort, not to mention the two infamous fighters and madmen, Captain Rackham and Captain Blackbeard.

Once the Black Knight was happy that Podge understood the plan and could recite it back to him, the two settled down at the treeline to wait. The sleeping pirate woke earlier than expected, around midnight, but another tap on the head sent him back to sleep. At around 4am, when the night was at its darkest and sleep at its deepest, two shadowy shapes moved forward from the tree line. Podge moved off to the right of the gates and disappeared amongst the shanty huts. In his hands he held the large satchel, from which protruded a long fuse wire. The Black Knight moved slowly through the shanty huts that lined the approach to the open gates of the fort.

He saw that an old wagon had been pulled in front of the gate as some kind of flimsy barrier and wondered again about the pirates laziness in not repairing their gates. As he passed the huts, moving like a wraith in the darkness, he heard the soft snores and grunts from sleeping men within and saw the dull glow of dying embers in the cooking fires.

When he reached the old wagon at the gates, the Black Knight was able to step around it easily. A pirate lay spread-eagled on his back in the body of the cart, fast asleep. The hiss of a cat from underneath the wagon made the Black Knight start in surprise and an edge of his chest plate scraped on the rusted metal band of the wagons edge.

"Who's that, who's there? It's not time yet…" mumbled the pirate in the wagon, struggling to sit up and rub his eyes simultaneously.

Striking like a snake, the Black Knight's dagger flashed out and the pirate slumped gently back into the wagon. This was no time to take prisoners. Once past the wagon the courtyard of the fort opened up before the Black Knight. Torched burned dimly in sconces and the remains of a bonfire glowed in the centre of the yard.

Bottles of every shape and size lay where they had been thrown and the Black Knight could see the huddled shapes of some sleeping pirates in the dusty ground. This certainly explained the singing and yelling they had heard coming from the fort earlier on.

Beyond the bonfire the small tower sat in darkness, with the exception of a light emanating from the topmost window of the narrow tower. That must be where his brother was being held. Moving faster now, the Black Knight reached the base of the tower, which sat to one side of the keep. Its stones sat crookedly and moss and lichen grew from numerous cracks, some so large that you could fit your fist into them. Looking upward, the Black Knight saw that the whole tower leaned toward him, as if a strong wind might finally topple it. A handhold was easy to find and the Black Knight began to climb, taking care to not let his breastplate touch the old stone.

When he reached the first open window of the tower he peaked over the sill and into the dark room beyond. It seemed empty. Hoisting himself into the room, the Black Knight crouched and listened. He heard no shout of alarm, no footsteps in the stairwell and no sound of anyone breathing within the room, thankfully. The door sat ajar and a dim light from without allowed the Black Knight to find his way across the room. He opened the door slightly and winced at the squeak given off by the rusting hinges.

Instantly he heard a cough from upstairs, followed by, "Shut it, you!"

He looked into the stairwell which ran in a spiral up the centre of the tower, with doorways running off it. The stairs below were pitch black whilst the light from the upper room glowed softly down the stairs and moss covered stone of the walls.

The Black Knight moved onto the stairs and moved quietly up them, easing the repeating crossbow from his shoulder and gently levering the cocking handle to load a bolt. When he reached the uppermost door of the tower he saw that it was half open, spilling light into the stairwell. Again, from inside, a cough sounded, with a rattle of chains.

"Right, think you're funny do you?" rasped a voice.

Footsteps moved within the room and the Black Knight heard a hiss of pain. In one fluid movement the Black Knight swung the door open with his foot and stepped into the room, swinging the crossbow up as he did. The pirate guard stood with his back to the door and was pulling his sword back from the bars of a small cell.

"Going to cough again are we? If you do, you'll get another poke and I won't be so gentle this time."

Blood dripped from the tip of the sword as the pirate turned away from the cell. His haggard face was covered with a short scraggly beard that did little to cover the ragged scar that ran from his chin to his ear, not to mention the pock marks of some disease. When his mouth dropped open in surprise at the tall knight standing in the doorway, with a crossbow aimed squarely at his chest, four brown teeth could be seen in the 'o' of shock his mouth formed. He was no coward though and his chest had inflated to yell a warning when the crossbow twanged and the pirate was flung backward against the wall next to the cell, staring in horror at the spreading red patch on his chest. His sword would have fallen to the floor in a clatter had not a hand shot from between the bars and plucked it from the air. The dead pirate sank to the floor of the cell without a sound.

The hand holding the pirate's sword withdrew and the figure stood and turned to the Black Knight.

"I was wondering when you'd show up, brother."

Chapter 12

The huge man stepped forward in his cell. His blonde hair was unkempt and a light beard had sprouted in his time in captivity. Bruises covered his face, suggesting that the pirates hadn't been too gentle with their captive. His light trousers and shirt were stained and ragged and blood seeped from his leg, where the deceased pirate had stabbed him.

Moving to the table the Black Knight scooped up the large key and opened the cell door, swinging it open.

"Sorry to have kept you waiting Max," he said dryly, as the White Knight hobbled out of the cell and sat down in the chair beside the table, pulling up his trouser leg to inspect the wound.

The White Knight looked up and smiled.

"Thank goodness you got here so fast Henry, I'm not sure I would have had much longer to live! How did you get here so fast anyway?! I only sent that eagle a week ago!"

Speaking quickly whilst the White Knight bound his leg with a strip of cloth torn from his sleeve, the Black Knight filled his brother in on all that happened since he left his castle on that stormy night.

"Draco!" exclaimed the White Knight. "You were lucky it was him in that volcano and not some other dragon. I know I tried to stop you heading off north to fight with those beasts, but now I'm glad you did!"

The Black Knight nodded "it was a risk alright, but without Draco's help it would've taken me another week or more to get here. Not to mention the fact that you were to be executed this very morning as they thought they had killed me when they sank the Dragon's Tooth."

The White Knight paled in the candlelight "I'm sorry for all of this Henry, I was stupid to let them get me and then draw you into this." He gestured toward the wooden box in the corner of the room and, when the Black Knight lifted it over to him, the White Knight opened it with a smile and began to pull his armour on before continuing.

"I was at Eagles Reach," the White Knight referred to his castle that sat high in the mountains "and got word by messenger that a nearby village was having trouble with a wolf that had taken some of their cattle. I didn't bother taking any of my men with me to deal with one wolf so I went alone."

The Black Knight rolled his eyes. His brothers trusting nature and kindness had got him in trouble before.

"When I reached the village it was deserted. However, there were red arrows painted on the cobblestones and they led to the church." The White Knight stopped to buckle his breastplate on and then reached for his sword belt. "Its doors had been chained and I heard the sound of crying and yelling from within. I started toward the doors but was stopped by a shout. It was Calico Jack. He told me that the church had been rigged with dynamite which one of his men would set off if I didn't surrender." The White Knight grimaced at the memory "I had no choice brother. They made me take off my armour and sword and then they clapped me in chains and took me to the Ranger. I heard the sound of the church exploding as we left." The White Knight's face clouded in sadness.

The Black Knight saw that this had been a perfect plan to catch his brother. He would never have endangered the villagers.

The White Knight was ready for action; his armour shone in the candlelight, pure white and gleaming, seemingly unstainable. The huge doublehanded sword was strapped to the White Knight's back and its white leather handle poked from behind his brothers head. The armour seemed to almost glow and had been like that since the White Knight had been struck by lightning at the Battle of Eagles Reach. He had been wearing his usual armour and, instead of being killed instantly, the strike had transformed his armour so that when he got back to his feet it glowed white . Now, as the Black Knight watched, the bruises on the White Knight's face began to fade and the cut on his forehead started to knit together. Such was the power of his armour. Putting on his helmet he said, "Right, let's get out of here."

The two knights headed for the door, the Black Knight going in front, with his crossbow fully loaded and at the ready. As soon as he entered the stairwell he came face to face with a pirate boy, who dropped the tankard of beer he had been carrying with a clatter. It bounced down the stairs and the boy was so shocked at seeing two armed knights in the dark stairwell that he lost his footing and tumbled down the narrow stairs after the tankard, howling as he went. When he reached the bottom he began screeching.

"Help, help, the knight has escaped!"

The Black Knight and White Knight turned to each other "Looks like we do this the hard way, Max," said the Black Knight.

Outside, amidst the hubbub and running feet, the two knights heard a bellow.

"Quiiiieeettt."

Instantly, all was silent. The same voice called up the tower.

"Little pigs, little pigs, won't you come out?" A gale of laughter swept the pirates in the courtyard. The Black Knight peeked round the windowsill in the upper room and saw the gathering pirates and the two figures standing at their head.

"It's them, Blackbeard and Rackham, with at least 30 of their crew."

The booming voice echoed around the courtyard again.

"Or do I have to come in and get you?"

Out in the courtyard the pirate crews hooted with laughter behind the two men.

"I don't know how you survived my little surprise at the island, knight, but I'm glad I get to kill you and your brother at the same time." Blackbeard threw back his head and laughed. Beside him, Captain Rackham smirked, his pencil thin moustache rising at either side of his mouth.

The door to the tower burst open as the Black Knight and the White Knight charged out of it, side by side, running toward the pirate crowd.

Recovering quickly from their initial surprise, the pirate crews hefted their assortment of cutlasses, axes and pikes and charged, streaming around the remains of the bonfire and leaving their captains standing at the edge of the fire. The first pirate to reach the knights held a battle-axe that he swung in a wide arc towards the White Knight. The White Knight ducked under the swing and jabbed his sword at the man's chest, feeling it go in, and the man fall. A bearded pirate with a frayed eyepatch leapt toward the Black Knight, slashing his cutlass at the knight's head and losing his own when the Black Knight knocked his sword aside easily with the dagger in his left hand before the great sword came cleaving in at the pirates neck. Two more pirates darted in at the Black Knight and three came at once toward the White Knight.

Suddenly, the brothers were fighting for their lives, fending off blows from all directions, whilst more pirates hovered out of reach, waiting for an opening. Soon enough, the pirates' swords started making contact with the armour and every second a clanging noise or a rasping scrape sounded. The bodies of dead pirates began to collect around the knights' feet, but still more waited to replace their dead comrades. The Black Knight could feel blood trickling down his leg from where a cutlass point had found a gap in the armour and his sword arm felt like lead. The White Knight's armour was constantly healing him, but he, too, was tiring. Suddenly, a tattooed hulk of a pirate with a shaved head and gold teeth lunged toward the Black Knight from behind, catching him unaware. The pirate swung a battle hammer toward the Black Knight's legs, sweeping him off his feet to land with a thud on his back.

The pirate stepped over him, hefting the hammer above his head to bring it down on the Black Knight with all his strength. The Black Knight's breath had been driven from his body by the fall and he struggled to lift his sword to stop the hammer which came crashing down on his breastplate, ringing it like a bell and jarring the Black Knight's senses. The White Knight, hearing the crash, turned and, as the bald pirate lifted the hammer to strike again, leapt over the Black Knight and brought his sword down on the pirates shoulder, kicking the body away as it fell. The White Knight, standing over his brother, swung his sword in great arcs, driving the pirates back a few paces towards the embers of the fire and giving the Black Knight time to struggle to his feet. The Black Knight unslung the crossbow from his shoulder and began to fire into the crowd of twenty pirates that were left.

The six bolts were fired with the cocking handle crashing back and forth as the Black Knight sighted target after target. The pile of bodies had grown by the time he lowered the weapon. The rest of the pirates looked on in horror at the sudden death of so many and hesitated about pressing forward again. They had lost more than half their number to these bloodstained warriors.

"Don't kill them yet lads, give us a go!" A shout came from the gate of the fort. Ten fresh pirates trotted into the courtyard, obviously having arrived from the harbour. A fatter figure than most darted in from the side to join them. Cutlasses drawn, and grinning in anticipation, they moved past Blackbeard and Hook and joined their crew mates. Nearly thirty pirates faced the brothers again, who were already tired and nearing their limit.

Chapter 13

"I'm sorry you had to come here, Henry," whispered the White Knight.

Inside his helmet, the Black Knight was trying to regain his breath in readiness. "Oh, I wouldn't count us out yet, Max. Get ready to hit the deck." The White Knight saw his brother's teeth bared in a grin in the slit between the Black Knight's cheek guards.

Captain Rackham stepped forward with Blackbeard, coming around the fire towards their crew. Seeing the chance, the Black Knight yelled "NOW!" and flung himself toward the White Knight, bringing him to the ground.

The portly figure that had joined the fresh pirates darted forward and hefted a leather satchel towards the fire, hitting it right in the centre. He then ran faster than his size would suggest was possible in the opposite direction.

The satchel lay in the fire for a few seconds, with pirates staring at it dumbfounded. Rackham darted behind Blackbeard and Blackbeard moved like quicksilver as well, belying his bulk, and grabbed the collars of two of his own men, yanking them in front of him.

The gunpowder in the satchel went off with a bang that shook the walls of the fort and picked the pirates up as if they were dolls, flinging them around the courtyard to land in crumpled heaps. Blackbeard and Rackham were protected by the bodies of the two men Blackbeard had grabbed to use as human shields. They were still thrown backwards violently, landing in a tangle of furious pirate captains. The Black Knight and his brother had hit the ground and the fury of the explosion had blown over their heads. They got to their feet shakily and surveyed the scene of destruction. The pirate crews had been wiped out. Podge poked his head round the gate.

"My Lords!" he called, seeing them standing in the smoke filled courtyard, "it worked!"

"Well done, Podge," called the Black Knight. The plan he had devised had worked perfectly. Well, almost perfectly; the tangle of Blackbeard and Rackham was still moving.

The huge bulk of Captain Blackbeard began to rise from the ground, throwing the bodies of the two dead pirates of him like a dog shakes off ticks. Reaching down, he picked up Captain Rackham, who was a little less steady on his feet. The four men faced each other.

"It comes to this," the White Knight said. They came at a run, Blackbeard drawing a wickedly curved cutlass that caught the light of the rising sun, and Rackham a pace behind him, drawing a beautiful rapier.

"Let's finish this," snarled the Black Knight, and the brothers stepped forward, swords ready. There was no need for further words. When Blackbeard's sword crashed against the Black Knight's, the force of it drove him back a step but he rallied quickly, sending a blinding flurry of strikes at the huge captain, who countered with similar speed. Beside them, the White Knight and Rackham were exchanging blows, each looking for a weakness in the other's defence and testing their opponents defence. Theirs was a more considered fight than the fury of the clash between the other two combatants. Blackbeard lunged forward with a swinging cut that the Black Knight only just managed to deflect, the great cutlass scraping a shower of sparks against the Black Knight's armour as it passed. With his mountainous shoulder, Blackbeard shoved the Black Knight, who, exhausted, stumbled backward. The next blow from Blackbeard almost knocked the sword from the Black Knight's hand and he stumbled back again. Blackbeard's sword lunged forward, but met only air as the Black Knight stepped sideways and slammed a fist against the huge pirates temple. This would have knocked any other man out cold. Momentarily stunned, Blackbeard moved on a few paces with the momentum of his lunge and shook his head to clear it. He was just fast enough to raise his cutlass to parry the Black Knight's sword as it flew down toward his neck.

Podge had watched the aftermath of the explosion and the four men beginning their fight in the courtyard. He removed two of the finely balanced throwing knives from the row strung across his chest and waited for an opportunity to strike. Before and opportunity presented itself, Podge heard the sound of distant voices behind him, coming from the direction of the harbour. Of course! The rest of the crew of the Bonecrusher and the Ranger! Podge couldn't warn the knights as they were locked in combat. What could he do?

Sheathing the knives, Podge grabbed a torch from the nearest sconce and rushed to the nearest shanty huts by the gates and began to play the torch at the ends of the palm frond roofs. The fire caught immediately and spread rapidly.

The shapes of the advancing pirates were hazy through the spreading smoke. Podge moved from hut to hut, and soon a dozen were ablaze, sending a thick plume of smoke drifting toward the harbour. Podge then grabbed a handful of fronds and ignited them under the old wagon in the gateway of the fortress. Satisfied that it was burning merrily, he entered the courtyard and spied the crossbow which the Black Knight had dropped. It was empty, but Podge had fresh bolts in a quiver on his belt. As he rushed to the crossbow and began reloading it, the Black Knight and White Knight fought on, trading blows with the pirates. Blackbeard showed no signs of tiring and, laughing, hammered blow after blow at the Black Knight, who was bleeding from more wounds by this stage. The White Knight, though still weak after his imprisonment, was holding his own against Rackham, the two evenly matched in skill.

Shouts rang from outside the fortress as the pirates tried to find a way past the flames.

"Get water now!" a voice called.

Suddenly, Captain Blackbeard swung a blow so hard that the Black Knight's sword snapped cleanly in two. His next blow narrowly missed the Black Knight, who jumped back to avoid it.

"My Lord!" screamed Podge and tossed the crossbow.

The Black Knight caught it cleanly and brought it up, firing a bolt point blank into the snarling Blackbeard's chest. Blackbeard didn't stop and swung his sword again, catching the breastplate of the Black Knight's armour in a glancing blow. The crossbow fired again. And a third time. The bolts showed little sign of stopping the mountain of man who still came on, backing the Black Knight into a corner of the courtyard. The fourth bolt made Blackbeard check and the Black Knight took his chance and, drawing his dagger, leapt at the pirate, sinking his dagger into Blackbeard's black heart. The huge man sighed and sank to the ground.

Chapter 14

Seeing Blackbeard fall, Jack Rackham whirled on his heel and raced toward the blazing wagon. He hurdled it in one stride and was gone, through the flames.

Hearing the increased clamour beyond the burning wagon, the White Knight turned to his brother and Podge.

"We need to get out of here before Rackham makes them get past that wagon. Come on!"

He led the way at a run toward the tower where he had been imprisoned and scooped up a coil of rope that lay in the courtyard. The Black Knight dropped the crossbow and lifted Blackbeard's sword that had fallen from his senseless fingers. The three raced up the steps. A shout in the courtyard below revealed that the pirates had broken through and were into the fortress, Captain Rackham at their head, looking only slightly singed but extremely angry.

The White Knight directed Podge to start throwing furniture and anything he could get his hands on down the spiral stairs to block the pirates. He then tied the rope to his sword to form a grappling hook of sorts and hurled it out of the window and over the battlements of the outer wall. Securing one end to the upper bars of his cell, he tested the rope.

"Let's hope this holds!" he said, picking up a chair and snapping off one of the legs. He bodily lifted Podge to the narrow windowsill and showed him how to hook the chair leg over the rope and hold each side with both hands.

"You'll get a bit of rope burn, but whatever you do, don't let go," murmured the White Knight. With a gently prod he encouraged Podge to let the rope take his weight. The rope sagged but held, and a shove in the back sent Podge sliding toward the battlements. He landed in an untidy heap on the wall and looked back to the tower window. The White Knight gestured his brother forward to the window as the shouts began to echo up the stairwell. The pirates had figured out where the three men had gone.

"Go! I'll be right behind you," snarled the Black Knight over his shoulder. He faced the door of the room with Blackbeard's sword held ready. The White Knight knew not to argue with his stubborn brother and exited the tower on the rope. When the Black Knight had followed and landed safely, the three looked over the edge of the wall. Below lay an uninviting sight; the scrap pile from the fortresses kitchens. A midden of old food scraps and all the rubbish of the day had built up, disgorged here by a small hole in the wall, behind which lay the kitchen.

"It'll have to do," muttered the Black Knight and, grabbing Podge, hopped over the battlements. He landed with a squelch and was spattered with ooze when his brother landed beside them.

The three clambered off the midden and made off in the direction of the harbour. Behind them, the pirates clawed and hacked at the blockage in the staircase, not realising that their quarry had flown.

It took the two knights and Podge a little over twenty minutes to reach the harbour and, as they crested a small sand dune, the moon emerged from behind a drifting cloud, making Podge gasp. There, sitting empty, were the Ranger and the Bonecrusher. All the pirates had clearly made for the fort at the sound of the explosion and the harbour lay empty, bottles strewn on the quayside, and seagulls landing to pick over discarded meals.

"Well gentlemen, choose your ship," laughed the White Knight.

"Bonecrusher," said both the Black Knight and Podge together.

The three ran for the gangplank and entered the impressive ship.

"Check that cannon." The Black Knight pointed to one of Bonecrusher's massive cannons that faced the Ranger. He dearly hoped it was loaded. Podge gave the thumbs up when he saw it was and then watched whilst the Black Knight squinted along the barrel. It would have to do. The Black Knight stood back and motioned Podge forward with the burning taper he had lit from a brazier on deck that the crew had been using to cook over before they had left in such a hurry.

"Fire!"

The cannon boomed and recoiled with a jerk. The ball nicked the mast of the Ranger just above the level of the shrouds. The Black Knight's heart sank. If this didn't work then they faced a chasing Ranger full of vengeful pirates. There was only one outcome in that scenario as the three men could not hope to sail the Bonecrusher to anything near its full potential, much less hold off a boarding party. He had just turned away from the Ranger when a crackling sound made him whirl. The main mast of the Ranger began to lean, cracking and creaking as it gathered momentum. With a crash, the mast collapsed onto the deck, smashing the wheel to smithereens.

"I couldn't have done that much better myself." The White Knight clapped his brother on the shoulder.

"Let's get this beast on the move before Rackham figures out we aren't still in that tower and comes to investigate with fifty more of his lads!" warned the Black Knight, "I'm not sure I fancy any more fighting today." Blood was still trickling from underneath his armour.

With a sail rigged and the lines cut, the huge ship made its way ponderously away from the harbour and out into the Dark Seas.

"We'll need to stop at the nearest port and pick up some new crew for this thing," remarked the White Knight. The ship was vastly too large for three men to crew.

Behind them on the shore, an enraged Captain Rackham crested the same sand dune that lead to the harbour and took in the scene in the moonlight. The mixture of the Ranger's crew and those of Bonecrusher's weren't far behind and groaned as they saw the damage to the Ranger and the escaping knights waving at them from Bonecrusher.

Captain Rackham let rip a scream of pure fury and yelled "I'll get you! If it's the last thing I do, I'll get you!" he waved a fist impotently as the laughter of the brothers reached him.

With enough sails set to power the big ship, the Bonecrusher started to pick up speed and leave Skull Island behind. Podge busied himself searching for some food for the small crew whilst the knights stood at the helm, the White Knight guiding the Bonecrusher out into open water.

"Maybe we should team up more often?" The Black Knight said, as he removed his helmet and let the sweat dry from his hair. He began to unbuckle his armour, wincing as it came away.

"I can't argue with you there, Henry!" his brother replied.

"Glad to hear it." Grinned the Black Knight. "In fact, I may have a mission for us in the Far North."

"Of course, you do." Max rolled his eyes.

The Bonecrusher sailed west, heading for the Black Gates and home. For now.